# Seawind

## M. Blackwell

*Table of Contents*

*Once upon a time, there was a storm.....as sea and wind raged and tore at earth and sky, a solitary, three-masted ship was driven inexorably towards that familiar, treacherous shore.*

# 1. Driftwood

It all began with her first glimpse of the Inn in the gathering October twilight. With its gables, weathered shingles and peeling paint, surrounded by spooky trees, Sam should have known it meant trouble and stayed away. But that would have been making things too easy. She was lost once again, in the little villages mid-Cape, trying to find her way to the Mall at Hyannis. A wrong turn brought her to a quiet, empty road, which seemed to be heading to the shore, then at the last moment twisted away and petered out in front of the house. Despite the peeling pistachio green paint and general air of neglect, it had a gaunt sort of charm. A small, nearly invisible sign in front hanging from a dwarf apple tree read: Seawind.

As she parked and got out to look for somebody to give directions, bloodcurdling screams erupted from within. For a moment she froze. Then, always willing to help her fellow creatures, she made a dash for the front door. Stumbling through a dimly lighted hallway into an immaculate if shabby living room, she found two old ladies with identical blue rinses watching American Idol. Their favorite had just been disqualified. As Sam struggled to catch her breath, relieved that the damage was non-sanguine, a small tornado hurled through the door and gradually resolved itself into a small, anxious looking woman with a quantity of curly hair getting into her eyes. She consoled her guests on their disappointment, nodded politely at Sam and sank heavily into a nearby armchair. Her eyes closed and she seemed to fall asleep instantly. Beth Cartwright, innkeeper.

Just then the front door slammed open and the clump of footsteps in the hallway spoke of more guests arriving. A second later, a sudden, ominous smell of singed food drifted into the room. "The casserole!" Beth woke, correctly identified the smell, and fled towards the rear of the house to deal with it. Trailing along behind Beth, Sam saw a kitchen with much to be done. From Beth's distracted comments, she learnt that the cook, offended in some mysterious way, had departed in the midst of dinner preparations, leaving her to do her inadequate best. Seizing the opportunity, Sam offered to help rescue dinner while Beth checked in the new guests. Four hours later, by the time they had finished serving a four-course dinner for ten, washing up, and setting the table for breakfast next morning, Sam had found herself a job.

The next morning she walked barefoot on the beach before heading in to work, congratulating herself on the lucky chance that brought them to the Cape instead of one of the struggling little postindustrial towns near the state line. The sea was like diamonds and the air warm and pure, the sand under her feet healing. "In this life, there are no coincidences," said a passing seagull, turning his head to look directly at her in the way seagulls do, as he flapped past lazily horizontal. How right he was.

Happily gathering seawrack - shells, seaweed and small stones - Sam found a small nearly rectangular piece of wood, weathered to a dark brown, with intriguing marks chiseled on it. She added it to her stash. She was building up quite a collection to display on the window sill of her attic room at the inn. Now, while she imagines herself to be in paradise, would be a good time to introduce our heroine: she is Samantha Black, an out-of-work anthropologist. Out of work until she came to Seawind, as kitchen help, dishwasher, runner of errands, maker of beds, and general dogsbody. And Sebastian - fifteen pounds, black velvet, pointy ears, whiskers - yes, he's a cat. And that rounds out the little household fleeing recession in the midwest to fetch up in Cape Cod in the autumn.

Beth had just taken up a new role as innkeeper. A distant aunt had died a year ago, and left her the house. Aunt Caroline, it appeared, had been the quintessential New England aunt, reserved, self reliant, and a real pack rat. At the end of her long eccentric life, she decided to leave her house and all it contained to her sister's granddaughter. This was Beth, whom she had last seen thirty years ago, as a querulous five-year old. Perhaps she felt their temperaments matched. Certainly there ran a streak of eccentricity, politely called impulsiveness, in the family. It was this trait that led Beth to quit her job as a successful public defender in New York city, and move to the Cape to take up her inheritance. Instead of selling the house, she had decided that it should become one of Cape Cod's landmark inns. Her lack of domestic and commercial ability did not bother her in the least, not in the beginning.

For one thing she was lucky enough to find a gifted cook, whose improvised menus kept the dining room full on weekends. Though he doubled as handyman and jazz guitar player, Phil had also acquired and cultivated a chef's sensibilities. He was given to storming out of the kitchen and the Inn if any ingredients were missing for one of his lavish and celebrated dishes. Since the shopping was his responsibility, and he insisted on relying on his none too perfect memory rather than written lists, these crises occurred with weekly regularity, though the day of the week varied. This made for a certain amount of instability in the menu, and also in interpersonal relationships. Phil's dog Daisy, a rescue mutt of  indeterminate color, however was a different matter. A wise dog if there ever was one, Daisy knew a good thing when she saw it and stayed on at Seawind each time Phil packed up his things and left in a huff in his red pickup truck. She knew he would be back at mealtimes, and meanwhile she much preferred the comfort of the inn to his bachelor quarters.

The house itself wore its age and history with an air of quiet dignity, despite its outwardly dilapidated appearance. The date over the front door read 1842, but the structure was basically sound, made to withstand centuries of storms. Square built with gables and a widow's walk, it followed no particular style but blended in with its surroundings, a typical Cape landscape of scrubby pines interspersed with oak, and the occasional apple tree, all well-adorned with grey-green lichens. The house and its surroundings needed more work and care than Beth and Phil could steal from the exigencies of inn keeping.

Inside, the worst excesses of generations of pack rats had been stowed away in the basement. The furniture that remained was charmingly mismatched and homely, the elegant and the comfortable agreeably blended over the years. The chandelier in the living room was an original, the chairs covered in flowered slipcovers and, frequently, dog hair. A long dim hallway had doors opening out on both sides into the living room, dining room, a morning room that also served as library, and a private study. The rooms were well-proportioned, and retained the original wide plank hardwood floors. At the very back were the kitchens and store rooms. Upstairs were four bedrooms with their newly renovated bathrooms, a narrow linen closet, and a door at the back of the landing that gave out on to the widow's walk that circled the house. Set back a little way from the house were the converted stables, now serving as living quarters for Beth and Phil.

On her first tour of the house Sam was offered a look at the basements, packed with furniture, boxes and trunks of intriguing shape and design. Looking at the hoard of mysterious shapes lurking in the dim light, they resolved to investigate these treasures at some convenient time in the future. "There's been absolutely no time to sort through all that stuff," Beth said regretfully, of the hoard in the basement, "for all we know there might be some valuable antiques there."

She wasn't sure that she would sell any that proved to be valuable, as they were not only antiques but also her family's history. Like many Cape families, Beth's forbears had been seafarers. Though the Cape itself was and is an oddly remote little corner of the northeast, the men who lived here had sailed to the corners of the earth. One of her most prized possessions was a small wooden box, pale green and inlaid with a design of silver Arabesques. It had been found in the attics, buried at the bottom of a wooden chest full of antique clothing. The silver clasp was also intricately carved, and to Beth's lasting chagrin the key had not been found. The green-and-silver box, precious and enigmatic, was displayed proudly on the mantel in the morning room. Beth had convinced herself there was something worth finding inside, though shaking it provided no clues to its contents; it appeared to be empty.

The spacious attics had been renovated along with  the rest of the house before the Inn opened. This was Samantha's domain: a small bedroom with a bathroom next to it, and across the landing, a large room that served as living room and play area for Sebastian. The large dormer windows had window-seats built in, low to the ground. The furniture was minimal, but comfortable and homely. Scattered rugs in faded pink, pale green and cream contrasted the colors of spring with the bare trees outside. Comfortable flowered cushions on the window seats made them Sebastian's favorite spot for napping. And there were built-in bookcases, painted antique cream like the walls, for the books that began to accumulate around Sam the moment she put down roots anywhere.

Sebastian and Daisy divided their time indoors between the attics and the kitchen. They took to each other right away, and established a pecking order which has always been part of the natural order of things; the cat as the superior aloof being and the dog his humble and devoted follower, except when stealing his food and his toys.

## 2. The Storm

October is Cape Cod's best kept secret. Samantha discovered that the weather was warm enough to spend her days off at the beach. The crowds were gone, and there were times when she could walk a mile or more on the beach on pristine sand, with no footprints but her own and the sandpipers' tracks. She and Sebastian rediscovered their old friend the Atlantic wind, which blew strongly day and night. They had missed it in the Midwest. The wind was Sebastian's old frenemy. He would jump and make cheerful little pounces at it until it tugged his ears and whiskers too fiercely, sending him running indoors for cover.

In geological terms the Cape could be described as a hook of sand running out forty miles east, then another forty to the north, into the Atlantic. It was yet another lands end, a mystical boundary of land, sea and sky. The desolate monochrome beauty of the Cape in the winter was a contrast to the frantic summer crowds and their accoutrements, which attempted to contain the place in the seaside tourist cliches of souvenir and t-shirt shops, mini golf courses and pirate-themed amusement parks. Like all mysteries, it too was deeply contaminated by the modern world. And yet, the mystery existed, not to be swallowed up in the cultural narratives of the pilgrims, horror movies, tourism or summertime.

Exploring the solitudes of the Cape, Sam recalled that Hopper had chosen to live here, in a house overlooking the the bare green hills of Truro. The pine barrens, salt marshes, bogs, ponds and meadows made for an eerie, desolate landscape that could not be scaled down to human terms. Hopper's  paintings  of the strangely matching emptiness of the Cape and New York City - she thought of his paintings of Queensborough Bridge and Corn Hill as somehow similar - pictured people lost in a physical environment which diminished human activity to the point of irrelevance. Whether natural or artificial, in both City and Cape the environment followed its own life and cycles of the year. They had purposes of their own, and it was not revealed to the humans wandering in and through these places what those purposes were. In the meantime, it was enough just to be there, to breathe the pine- and oak- scented air of the barrens and marvel at one's luck. The Inn backed on a hundred acres of woodland and state park, and it always amazed Sam that she could just walk of the front door to such an unspoilt place, and have it almost all to herself. The sandy tracks were covered in pine needles and perfect for running, walking, and getting lost in.

That the solitude of the Cape survived property developers was due to the creation of the National Seashore area in the 1960s, allowing the narrow land to recover from the depredations of centuries of deforestation. It was also due to the unique class structure, which priced out the middle class by the simple expedient of ensuring the near-absence of white collar jobs within a seventy-mile radius. Beth had had more time than Sam to observe this structure and had her own theories about it. What they lacked in sophistication, they made up in depth of feeling. She was wont to enlarge upon her ideas over a nightcap of Black Label. "Yobs and pats," she would say, waving her glass dangerously around, "that's all there's room for here. It's the same in all of Massachusetts, really. They're opposites but they need each other. The yobs need someone to look up to, and the pats...the pats..." she was really hitting her stride now, reflecting on her own patrician New England background, on her mother's side "...are horrified by the yobs, by the tattoos, the teen pregnancies, the drinks-and-drugs, but they need them to make themselves look better in comparison. What's an upper class, without the plebs? How do they feel superior if there's no one to feel superior to?"

What made it all the more confusing for Sam was that they all spoke with Massachusetts accents, which sounded cultivated and literate even when the speakers were not. The class structure was echoed in the houses, as well. Proximity to the water, naturally, was the differentiator. But there was also the more subtle matter of house construction and materials. The homes of the summer rich in Chatham were resolutely painted white each year, in contrast to the year-round houses of weathered cedar shingles. Now the summer houses were shuttered and empty, the roads were deserted and the shops shut down for the season. The Cape had come into it own.

Halloween was the night of the big storm and the high winds. For the first time in her life, Sam understood what people meant when they talked of hearing voices in the wind. And not nice voices either. There were howls, threats, evil intent, words and meaning on the very edge of reason. What would anyone see who looked out on the nightwind? Horses with manes flying, cloaked and hooded riders with birds of prey on shoulder and wrist, hounds baying for the kill? And before them fled screaming human souls, ragged, gasping, with bleeding feet, doomed always to be hunted. Following some instinct as old as Time, she knew not to look. A night to fear. Even as the wild hunt raged and whooped and howled outside, she dropped off into an uneasy sleep in the armchair in her attic living room.

This was not the Atlantic wind she and Sebastian knew so well. It had an edge that tested the limits of mortal endurance. And yet, for a while, the house itself was safe. Her sleep was interrupted several times by the howling wind. This was not a night for sleep, but reckoning. Puzzled and restless, for these thoughts came unbidden, Sam prowled around the room, wakened by the silence as the wind dropped off in the grey dawn. She noticed that her little collection of seawrack was looking a little different. The little oblong piece of wood had vanished, and in its place was a small pile of what looked like sawdust.

Though the next day dawned clear and bright, the storm had done its share of damage. The massive old oak at the head of the little track that ran behind and then east of the house had been hit by lightning. One of its primary branches lay burnt and twisted beside the tree. The tree itself had been so badly damaged that nearly half had to be cut away. A work crew with a cherry picker truck ringed the tree, and men wearing hard hats and reflective clothing were busy cordoning off the area. As the yellow tape fluttered in the breeze, the workers' chainsaws buzzed and bit deep into the wood. Samantha had a feeing of rising unease. The tree had been a giant sentinel, and now it was wounded, literally cut in half.

And indeed all was not well at Seawind. Indoors, she found Beth and Phil sitting at the desk in the morning room, grimly sorting through a pile of bills. The mail delivery had brought in another letter from the bank, raising the mortgage payment again.

"I thought your aunt left you the place," Even as she spoke, Sam was aware that her words would not comfort. Honesty was not alway the best policy, and she knew that she really had to work on that tendency of hers to speak without thinking.

Phil answered for Beth, "She did, but to pay for all the repairs, we had to take a mortgage on the house."

"Roof, heating and cooling systems and all windows replaced, two new bathrooms, the kitchen" Beth reeled off the list with mechanical ease. "I thought we would just recover the  money once the inn gets going, but it hasn't really."

"How did this happen to us? The mortgage was affordable when we started out." said Phil.

Sam knew how the story went. The bank had raised monthly payments until they ate up more than half the earnings. They were staring foreclosure in the face. This was the Cape's other secret. Its serene beauty harbored wrecks of many kinds. Nearly one in five people had lost a job or a house or both. Those lucky people, living by the seaside, walking their dogs along the trails covered in pine needles, and caring for their gardens full of late-blooming hydrangeas, were the walking wounded. A place of beauty and heartbreak.

Sam left them to it and went upstairs to her room.

# 3. An Appearance

Nauset was one great shout of a beach, mile upon mile of crashing water and wheeling seabirds, and a wind that blew stinging sand into your eyes and skin. A rainbow shimmered amid the spindrift. Despite the November cold, the surfers were out in the water. So were the children who succumbed to the water's invitation to come and play. They were being retrieved, wrapped in sweaters and hustled back shivering to the cars by their chilled parents. "They just jumped in!" a bemused mother with wind-reddened cheeks explained as Sam passed them on the steps leading down to the beach. At the bottom of the wooden steps, a large sign posted by the Fish and Wildlife Service informed visitors that seals were wild animals, should not be approached, and did not need to be covered with blankets or sweaters for comfort. The cold northern waters were, after their own fashion, full of life. The wild stretch of shore was home to a growing population of seals, which attracted both tourists and sharks. Inland were the cedar swamps and pine forests, the trees gnarled and twisted by the wind, weird and inexplicably beautiful.

The Inn was officially closed for the season, though the dining room continued to function as a highly popular restaurant. It was specially full on weekends, and Phil's brunches were famous. Unofficially, Eileen and Dori who had nowhere to go until the spring, continued to live in the two front rooms upstairs, which faced south and the winter sun. Their assisted living apartments would not be ready for occupancy until April, so Beth just allowed them to stay for a minimal rent. The innkeepers were also too softhearted  to turn away the stray travelers who regularly showed up at the Inn, drawn in some way to its appearance and location, or just plain lost. There was always work to be done, and diners on whom Phil could try out his new recipes.

Like most devoted Cape Codders, Phil was not a native but a transplant, from the Midwest. He had acquired his cooking skills in a bewildering variety of settings: dorm rooms, a horse farm, an apprenticeship at a high-end New York city restaurant, and a fishing boat galley featured among these. Eclectic but highly skilled, was the opinion of all who had the privilege of experiencing one of his meals. It was his enduring regret that of all foods, his favorite, an unpretentious caramel custard, eluded him. His periodic efforts to overcome this limitation left the kitchen littered with eggshells, patty pans, and little broken misshapen lumps of the most divine tasting custard. Try as he might, the little desserts would not stay whole. The residents of the Inn, human and animal, commiserated as they greedily consumed the delicious fragments. That evening a large family birthday party had taken over the dining room and spilled over into all the downstairs rooms. Beth and Sam were kept busy running around as Phil turned out bite sized crab cakes, stuffed mushrooms, hummus and pita for starters, before going on to a heroic meal that catered to the tastes of three generations. Black Forest gateau and coffee rounded off the menu and the chef's helpers thankfully began stacking the dishwasher for the last time.

Sam needed time to unwind before she could get to sleep after a hard day's work. She went out for a walk, tempted by the enormous golden hunter's moon that hung over the wounded old oak and cast clear shadows. It was early November and the world was turning towards winter. The bare trees and silent landscape, etched black and white in moonlight, were braced for the snows and storms of the season. That night she stayed up later than usual, caught up in the book she was reading. It seemed that the Cape prompted people to extremes. Personal memoirs were full of stories of people living in lonely houses on the edge of the water through winter storms, sailing in uncertain weather, braving hurricane force winds that according to one account would strip the paint from parked cars. People seeking isolation and danger and if they survived these, some form of understanding. Something in the environment called to itself the reckless, the foolhardy and the downright foolish. Sam wondered to which of these categories she belonged.

She read on, getting more and more tired, yet unwilling to seek her bed and sleep. Finally, around one o'clock, unable to keep her eyes open, she closed her book and stood up. The house was silent and asleep around her. She turned towards the door, and then paused. In that fleeting instant, something in the room changed. With its flowered curtains, French windows opening to the little rose garden at the side of the house, and book-covered walls, the morning room was  one of the most welcoming in the house. Now it felt cold as ice. She turned around and saw a dim, shadowy figure standing by the mantelpiece, one hand reaching out to the green and silver box so greatly prized by Beth.

Sam's first confused thought was "He must be in the wrong house." This was closely followed by a second, equally confused one: "He must be in the wrong century." For the figure was dressed in some kind of costume. As she looked, the shadow that seemed to surround the figure faded away, and she could see him clearly. Sam was not an expert on men's clothing but the dark grey frock coat, richly brocaded waistcoat with watch and chain, and arrogant stance all suggested the nineteenth century. It was the face, however, that  held her attention. Ugly but arresting, piercing eyes, confident, cruel, with sweeping eyebrows and an aggressive chin; once seen, it would not be easily forgotten.

It had been a calm night, but as Sam stood staring in disbelief at the figure appeared out of nowhere, a wind came screaming out of the night and hurled itself at the house, shaking the windows and shutters and rattling the light fixtures. Sam heard dimly, as if an echo of the wind, the howls and cries, and the distant sound of hoofbeats that she had heard on the night of the Halloween storm. The figure by the mantel heard them too. It turned, the face distorted into a snarl of hate and recognition. The French windows burst open and the wind rushed in, amid billowing curtains and a storm of paper. For a moment the room was full of chaos. Above the clamor of the wind, a distinct sound rose, blood-chilling but in some way human in origin, a cry of rage and despair. It came from the figure by the fireplace, which shrank and cowered away from the whirlwind gathering in the room. Then, abruptly, it flickered and vanished. For a moment longer, the wind raged through the room. Then, as if in pursuit of the shadow, it died away.

The silence that followed was broken only by a regular sharp sound, which Sam gradually recognized as her own breathing, coming in short gasps. She stood still for a long time, her hand upon the doorpost, unable to form any coherent thoughts. Her eyes told her that she had just seen a figure appear and disappear, but her mind had a hard time accepting the word she knew should describe it. Not that there was anything ghostly or insubstantial about the figure, but the cold air of evil and the fact that he had vanished before her eyes were unmistakable. Could she have been dreaming? She dismissed that thought as it arose. She was not given to dreams or hallucinations, had always prided herself on her clarity of thinking and insight. Her thoughts were interrupted by a low moaning noise, which proved to be Daisy. She had taken refuge behind the couch and was now stuck. As Sebastian's furry black face emerged cautiously from behind the cushions on the couch, Samantha set about the task of extricating Daisy and comforting her. She finally accepted a handful of treats and then followed Sebastian to the safety of the attics. Like most large dogs, she was an abysmal coward about thunderstorms and bad weather. Since she was too big to fit under beds, her favorite refuge in stormy weather was behind the couch in the attic living room, which Sam had thoughtfully pulled forward to make room for her.

Sufficiently distracted, Sam tried to set the room to rights, picking up books and papers and clearing away the remains of a shattered china ornament - an inoffensive rendering of a windjammer - that had been knocked off the bookshelves and smashed. She carefully closed the windows and examined the latches. They were undamaged, and in perfect condition, with nothing to indicate why they had given way before the wind. Then, with infinite reluctance, she slowly walked over to the mantelpiece where the figure had stood. There was no sign of the apparition, which had quickly become a dim if unpleasant memory. Gazing around the room, she could see no physical traces of its presence. She regarded the little green and silver box on the mantel with curiosity  and suspicion. Had it brought the ghost and its attendant storm to the house? And if it had, why? Was it changed in some way? The box continued to gleam a dull, pale green and

bright silver, and kept its secrets.


Surprisingly, the rest of the household had slept through the ruckus. Sam found sleep

elusive and only dozed off as the sky began to show the first light of dawn. She woke

late, unrefreshed, and rushed downstairs to find breakfast nearly over. Bringing in fresh

supplies of toast and coffee, she noticed in passing that Beth looked tired and unrested.

In fact, she looked exactly as Samantha herself felt. This was confirmed when Phil

bounced in an hour later, laden with groceries and full of plans for a new recipe for his

famed seafood ambrosia. They were grimly  engaged with the week's baking, and the

chaos of mixing dominated the kitchen. The air was heavy with unspoken questions

and explanations nobody wanted. There was a lot left unsaid and they were determined

to keep it that way.


Phil took one look at his ashen faced helpers and realized that serious matters were

afoot.

"What's been happening here?" he demanded,"both of you look as if you've just seen a

ghost!"

Beth's hands shook and she dropped the basket of eggs she was carrying from the

fridge to the large farm table that served as a working space in the center of the kitchen.

The resulting mess on the floor took a good quarter of an hour to clean, despite Daisy's good natured efforts to help. Phil took advantage of the confusion to add his own ingredients into the bread and cake mixes, though he had been sternly forbidden to do so. His cooking was inspired and improvised, turning out flawless and mouthwatering dishes with a minimum of effort. Beth by contrast cooked by the book and resisted all efforts at change. She pointedly removed the baking pans, now with a dubious scattering of raisins, dates and sunflower seeds that Phil was convinced belonged there, and heaved them into the oven.

"Now you have room for your seafood," she remarked, pulling off her apron and depositing it on top of Sebastian, asleep on one of the kitchen chairs. He gave a small sigh and snuggled into the impromptu blanket. But Phil was not to be deflected so easily, and returned to his question with Midwestern tenacity. He began sautéing seafood and his inquisition simultaneously. "Ghosts," he said, pointing his marinade brush at Beth and Sam, "Talk. Now."

"..." they began, then stopped and looked at each other.

"You've seen it, too," Sam said accusingly

Beth managed a weak smile.

"Not seen, exactly..."

"Why didn't you tell me?" demanded Sam.

"There's nothing to tell really," began Beth, "and I didn't see anything. Its just that for the past few days…"

They might have continued evading the subject for days, but were interrupted by Phil. After taking the pan of perfectly sizzled seafood off the cooker, he kindly but firmly steered them to the table and sat them down in the mismatched captains chairs. They were allowed to resume the conversation only when he had provided cups of coffee and almond Danishes for all three, and one for Daisy. Sebastian got two of the jumbo shrimp that were the key ingredient of the seafood ambrosia.

"Now that we're all fed," said Phil, "let's begin again. What ghosts?"

"You go first," said Sam, crumbling her uneaten danish in her plate.

"All right," said Beth, speaking slowly and carefully, "since I'm not even sure there is anything to tell. It's just that for about the past week or so, when I've been alone, I hear footsteps going up and down the stairs. Not just once or twice, but every time I'm alone in the house."

Her plain statement left them silent for a while. Even with the sunlight pouring in through the windows, Sam in her turn was curiously reluctant to speak of her own experience. She frowned at the dust motes dancing in a ray of light, searching for a way to put the events of the previous evening into words. Her memory of the Victorian figure standing by the fireplace was not one she wanted to dwell upon. The questioning and expectant looks on the others' faces forced her to frame the words she could scarcely bring herself to believe.

"I saw him," she said finally, ""and I'm quite sure I didn't imagine it. He looked like something out of a nineteenth century illustration - you know, what you'd expect to see in the *Strand Magazine*? And then he vanished."

This very inadequate account prompted a volley of questions from her listeners.

"Who?"

"Vanished?"

"How? When?"

"Which issue of the *Strand Magazine*?"

"Well, just that one moment he was there, and the next he was gone." Sam frowned at the memory, as she tried to keep track of their questions: "I think it may have been just as the wind rushed in. The doors and windows were flung open. The issues that originally serialized the Sherlock Holmes stories."

The baffled looks on her listeners' faces told her that she was not making any sense at all. She took a deep breath, and started again. As she forced herself to describe the unlikely sequence of events, she could see a pattern falling into place, one that matched her feelings about the events. The ghost had appeared, reached for Beth's prized silver and green box. Almost as if it sought and pursued him, the wind had come howling round the house as soon as he was clearly seen, and had vanished after him, as if in pursuit. The sturdy doors and windows could not have just opened by themselves. Phil had reinforced and reinstalled them and agreed that not even the  strongest wind could force them open. Cape houses were built to withstand Atlantic storms.


There was a long silence as the implications of Sam's narrative sank in. Phil was the first to recover: "Well, it seems that your ghosts are less retiring than Beth's."
Beth made an inarticulate sound of disagreement, which they understood to mean that the sounds she heard were not ghostly, nor were her ghosts in any way inferior to Sam's. Her denials went unheeded, but continued to punctuate the conversation.
"It's not a competition," Sam said indignantly, "not one I want to win, anyway!"
"So, it seems," Phil went on thoughtfully, ignoring her comment as well "we might have not just one but two spooks! The Victorian gentleman and the thing that opened the windows."
"Yes," agreed Sam, "and the strangest thing is that they had such a different feel. The ghost was just plain evil. And the wind....was...scary....but somehow, not bad. I really don't know how to explain it."
"Oh nonsense!" Beth had had enough of the conversation, "there's no such thing as ghosts! You've just been reading  too many stories."

"You should talk," said Phil "you've just finished telling us about the ghostly footsteps you hear in the house!"

"But!" began Beth again, "that could be just anything!" She was however fighting a losing battle, not against Phil's counter-arguments but her own memory of the encounters.

"See, for some reason they frighten you," Sam, said more sympathetically. "I don't believe in ghosts either, but I'm not willing to doubt the evidence of my own senses. And I certainly didn't imagine the cold air and the feel of evil in the room."

As Beth fell silent, it was clear she had not only heard but sensed the ghost. The sense of evil was the strongest sign of its presence.

# 4. Good Spirits

Though they quickly settled into the roles of believer, rationalist and agnostic, their different responses to the ghost produced the same results. The morning room began to wear a deserted look. Beth, who prided herself on her practical, rationalist New England Yankee heritage, persisted in refusing to believe in ghosts. But she took great pains to not be alone in the house or the morning room again. She didn't believe in ghosts, she insisted, but admitted to being terrified of them. Sam found herself struggling to retain her academic and scientific detachment and decided to research Cape ghosts. Phil and the animals were just plain afraid and refused to go into the morning room at all.

As she went through the rounds of work at the Inn, Sam's thoughts kept returning to her memory of that evening. Were there really two different ghosts, as Phil suggested? The Victorian figure and the wind, or the Hunt, as she thought of it, had had a completely different feeling, though each was unearthly and terrifying in its own way. The ghost felt evil, and Sam had seen enough of it in her career studying violence to recognize the bedrock of implacable hatred. The Hunt, by contrast, while utterly terrifying, felt like a primal force of nature. "Like a shark," she thought, "but somehow moral." And she could have sworn that they were opposed to each other. The antagonism of the wind had been almost tangible, and the ghost had clearly fled before it. What was it about the wind that could reduce an evil spirit to such terror? The mystery began to occupy all her waking  hours. Work was now an escape as well as a duty for all of them, and Sam began some long overdue cleaning projects. As a self confessed lifelong nerd, her first project was the bookshelves in the morning room, with their motley collection of books accumulated over five generations.

"I don't understand," mused Sam, as she plied her duster, "why here, of all places? What would bring all these - things" she forced herself to say, "these...spirits...what would bring all these things to such a quiet out-of-the-way place, which already has some kind  of enchantment of its own?"

Unconsciously, she had spoken aloud. She found that she had an audience. Eileen and Dori stood in the doorway, fixing her with identical stares. Sam had discovered that their resemblance to each other was a matter not of feature but expression.

"Did you say 'spirits', dear?" asked Dori "have you seen them too?"

It was Sam's turn to stare.

"Do you mean to say that you've seen him too?" she demanded.

Eileen and Dori took on purposefully vague expressions, which Sam recognized as a stalling tactic. They were far from amnesiac but sometimes found it convenient to pretend to be suffering from memory loss. Sam flicked her duster from hand to hand pointedly, and waited.

Finally Eileen mumbled, "Well, you see, we didn't want to worry you young folks…" Sam forebore to mention that in this case, young was only a relative term. She also decided not to mention that Beth had cautioned her against talking about the ghosts to the two old ladies, because "It would only worry the poor old dears." In fact the old dears, as Sam had discovered over time, while certainly tending towards indigence, were tough as old boots, and militant defenders of the fast vanishing civil liberties of the realm. They took their positions as retired school teacher and librarian respectively very seriously, and penned letters of exquisite outrage and composition to the local newspaper with each new revelation of online surveillance and government misconduct. They took supernatural manifestations in their stride, and had a few interesting observations to make on the nature of the ghost.

"He's not a local," said Dori, shaking her head decisively, "Cape ghosts are polite, gentle folks, meaning no one any harm. They're mostly just apologetic for wanting to revisit their former homes."

"And sometimes curious to look at the new people living there. Now this….thing," said Eileen thoughtfully, "is not apologetic about being found in someone else's house. The mark of a thief."

Sam could only agree heartily, while marveling at the ease with which they accepted the fact and presence of the manifestation.

Though well versed in the lore of Cape ghosts, they too were not natives but transplants from Florida, reverse snowbirds, in a sense. She was very glad of their sound common sense approach to the manifestations, and decided to model her attitude on their astringent intellectual view of supernatural phenomena. This resolve led her to delve deeper into accounts of ghost sightings on the Cape. These, she discovered, were legion. Cape residents took the idea and actual manifestation of spirits in a rather casual, everyday fashion. Very few actually doubted their existence, but Sam was disappointed to learn that Dori and Eileen had been right in their assessment of Cape ghosts. They were almost uniformly reported to be rather shy, gentle creatures, almost like a guardian spirit watching over the new inhabitants of the houses in which  they had lived. They tended to appear when a house had new owners, or when repairs or restoration work were done in old houses, their presence nothing more than a benign interest in the new inhabitants and their activity. A far cry from the arrogant and cruel late Victorian apparition that had materialized in the morning room.

Following Eileen's excellent advice, she addressed herself to the fundamental questions: Why here? Why now? What was it about the house and its inhabitants that drew the spirit and the pursuing hunt? Thoroughly intrigued, Sam decided that it was necessary to investigate the history  of the house and the family that had lived there. Though she told herself it was her academic training, now almost an instinct, that prompted her research, subconsciously she was aware that a greater force guiding her was her guilty fondness for the mock gothic. Her favorite writer was Barbara Michaels, not least because each time her motley characters went on the lam to escape evil spirits or bad guys, they remembered to bring their pets with them, the cats safely ensconced in their carriers. It had been a sad day for Sam when she concluded that she had read all Michael' books. That afternoon, Sam recalled that there was an old family Bible in the morning room. Laying aside her duster, she went in search of it, and found it as expected, on the rosewood Queen Anne bureau in the morning room. Opening it, Sam found her faith in American mock-gothic fully justified.

There, on the family record pages, was the history of the Cartwright family, tracing the descendants of Joseph Cartwright who had migrated from Scarborough in the North Riding of Yorkshire to Jamestown in Rhode Island, in the early years of the Industrial Age. He had lived to be eighty, and had fathered eight children of whom only five survived infancy. But it was not the grim notation of dates recording the deaths of the children that arrested Sam's attention. Joseph's second son Edward Cartwright had also met an untimely end at the age of thirty-two, on February 9, 1882. Abandoning the custom and form of recording only dates in the book, great emotion had impelled the writer to add anguished words beside the name.

*"Dear Heart we are sorely bereft - how much have you suffered! We are lost without your steadfast hand to guide us. Surely we shall meet some day in a happier place."*

The names of his widow and orphaned children were given as Lucinda, Marie and the infant Charles.


Clearly some great misfortune had befallen the family at that time, but there were no hints to its nature. They would have to find some other way to discover the history of the Cartwright family in 1882 and surrounding years. But Beth turned out to be no help. She had no knowledge of her family's history, nor why there might be a ghost in the house. She did however add the unknown history of the house to her list of things to worry about, along with the mortgage and the ghost that she would not admit was a ghost. Phil had no doubt that the answers lay in the history of the house, and that Sam was the right person to discover that history.

"Yer th' pr'fssr," he said, in a dreadful fake Cockney accent he had picked up from a public television show, "yer des the findin' out."

Sam shuddered and continued washing dishes that had the remains of a delicious lamb moussaka firmly adhering to the edges.

Her second instinct, as a trained anthropologist, was to ask the natives.

"Who might know the history of the house," she wondered aloud, "local historians? Folklorists?"

"Priests?" offered Phil, "specially if there have been any exorcisms done or requested."

"No priests," said Beth firmly "and definitely no exorcisms in my house. Past, present or future." And that was that for the time being.

The next time Sam found a clue to the history of the house, it was in a dream.

# 5. The Dream

Beaches and lighthouses were Cape icons. In Chatham they came with undertones of something that belied the holiday-by-the-sea gimcrackery of Main Street. The waters off Chatham Sands had currents and undertows that could pull an unwary swimmer under in a split second. The Sands themselves changed and shifted and had for hundreds of years made this stretch of coast dangerous for the shipping that was its livelihood. The sea constantly rearranged the coastline, and ate into the shore. It had carried off the predecessor to the lighthouse now in service, which had been moved back twice to keep it from the encroaching sea.

Sam had felt compelled to visit the Sands, drawn by their notoriety. Up close, the lighthouse was rather prosaic, squat and inconspicuous rather than tall and imposing, but the sands lived up to their promise. At low tide, it was possible to walk far out over the flat sands, but one had to be careful about the returning tide. Visitors were warned that swimming was forbidden because of the dangerous rip currents created by the shifting sands. That evening, sea and sky were arrayed in shades of twilight blue. The big golden moon hung low in the sky, its edges slightly blurred by clouds. This surreal landscape had a dangerous beauty. Somewhere out  there, she knew, were the great white sharks, tireless predators beyond human ken.

That night, Sam dreamt. In the dream, too, it was night. A storm raged on sea and land, throwing up walls of ragged water and foam. Flashes of lightning lit up the dark like screams, the wind howled and tore at all it could reach. Out on the shoal a ship foundered, her sails ragged and torn to shreds. There was no sign of any living thing, but the air of absolute evil that pervaded the scene had nothing to do with the storm. Another flash of lightning showed a dark mass, a body huddled on the beach. The afterimage of the lightning shed an eerie blue light on the scene. The rain beat mercilessly down. Sam saw the huddled figure move slightly, attempting to sit up. Injured, not dead.

Sam unconsciously twisted and turned in her sleep, tossing her head from side to side to break free from the spell of the nightmare. The dream continued. As she watched, unable to look away, another form approached the unconscious figure on the beach. Somehow, she knew that he was not there to help the stricken man. Heedless of the rain and storm, he went down on his knees and began searching the other's pockets with frantic haste. Finding something that appeared to be a piece of paper, he thrust it carelessly in his own pocket. He resumed the search, grappling and turning the injured body callously. His hands closed on something around the neck, and pulled. The object, whatever it was, came away in his hands. As Sam watched in horror, he gloated over it for a while before carefully stowing it away in an inside pocket of the greatcoat he wore under the oilskins. Then he stood and with great deliberation chose a heavy spar from the wreckage cast up on the beach. Swinging it with both hands like a club, he smashed it down again and again on the unconscious figure. A dark stain began to spread on the sand and into the gradually encroaching waves. Another flash of lightning lit up the attacker's face, twisted with the manic joy of killing. Samantha recognized him instantly. It was the ghost.

The next afternoon, as soon as she had finished her chores, Sam drove down to the public library. It was a Victorian building of dark red brick, with turrets rising at the four corners. The door was of solid oak, six inches thick. With its with curved iron clasps and knocker in the shape of a lion's head, it would not have disgraced a medieval castle. Finding the local history section, she began methodically and grimly pulling out books on storms and shipwrecks. There were a lot of these.

Back home, she settled down defiantly in the morning room with the stack of books at her elbow and a mug of Ovaltine. This stretch of the coast, she read, was known as the graveyard of the Atlantic. Since the first recorded shipwreck in 1626, the *Sparrowhawk*, there had been over a thousand ships lost on those forty miles. The vicious storms drove ships, specially in the days before steam, onto the shore where the shallow, shifting shoals became death traps. The sands were always changing, and there were no permanent channels to be memorized by the ships' pilots. Maps were outdated as soon as they were made, and there were no guides to navigate by.

Staring moodily out of the window she realized the books were telling her what she had begun to suspect from her walks along the Atlantic beaches. It was a mean, grey-green, wild, secretive body of water with a great appetite for both the living and the dead, human and nonhuman. Moral categories such as good and bad could not apply to such a primal force. She returned to the books, this time picking one with pictures. She opened it at random, and then stopped. There, on the page in front of her, was the ship she had dreamt. There was no doubt about it. The caption gave it a name and a date: *Seawind,* built in Maine in 1874. Run aground at Chatham during a storm in 1882, all forty crew and six officers were lost.

It could not be a coincidence that the name of the ship matched the house, and the date of its sinking was the same as the day of sorrow recorded in the family Bible. Sam couldn't bring herself to tell the others about her dream, but the unanswered questions chased each other around in her brain. What were the connections? Who was the ghost? Who was the injured man on the beach? Was it the Edmund Cartwright whose death was so pitifully mourned, one of Beth's seafaring ancestors?

# 6. The Folklorist

In the days that followed, the inn appeared to be truly haunted. No longer confined to the morning room or ghostly footsteps, the murderous spirit and its pursuing storm made a couple of brief appearances in the dining room at mealtimes. The first of these fortunately coincided with a private twenty-five year high school reunion, in its late stages of inebriety, and the ruckus caused by the ghost and Hunt was barely noticed amid the general disorder. The next time, however, it happened at lunchtime, when only a couple of tables were occupied. The guests, dispiritedly discussing real estate over Sam's excellent martinis - a hitherto undiscovered talent that she was finding very useful - were treated to a face-to-face encounter with the Victorian gentleman. He appeared in the middle of the room just as their first course was being served, walked to the nearest wall, and right through it. His departure was followed by the guests'. Torn between disbelief, fear and politeness, they abandoned their napkins and drinks, and mumbling inarticulate apologies, almost ran from the house. But they doubtless talked about it later, because the dining room suddenly saw a rush of customers, who took to walking around the inn and tapping on walls after they had finished their meals. Phil took it in his stride, glad to have more tasters for his culinary experimentation, but Beth began to dread the next appearance. A busy kitchen was not enough to compensate for the rumors that were starting to spread about Seawind. She did not want to be the owner of a *haunted* inn.

The problem solved itself, as problems often do, by transforming into something different, bigger and moving to a different location. This manifestation was witnessed by Phil and Daisy, and left them terrified and exhilarated.
"They chased him off!" He recalled for the others' benefit, later, "I don't know how they did it, but they just chased him out of the house. I even saw it happen."

The Victorian apparition, it seemed, had materialized in the kitchen, right beside Phil when he was completing his preparations for the perfect lamb pot roast. As the onions and rosemary for the glaze sizzled, Phil felt a sudden cold blast of air at his shoulder and turned to find himself almost nose to nose with the ghost. It says something for Phil's dedication to his art that he rescued the glaze from the stove before considering what to do next. Indeed, the ghost was forced to step backwards to accommodate Phil's maneuvering with the large sautéing pan. This involuntary two-step may have been the ghost's undoing. Distracted by the cookware thrust at him and Daisy's menacing barks from under the kitchen table, he missed seeing the pursuing wind, which broke screaming in through the kitchen windows.

"It lifted him," Phil recounted later, "and hurled him out through the window. Have you ever seem a human figure go right through glass and brick?!"

"Apart from the movies, you mean," said Beth, envy warring with and disbelief in her tone. For some obscure reason, Phil's nonchalance in the face of the supernatural annoyed her.

The results however were real. The spirit had been driven from the house, and even Beth began to relax. The morning after the last manifestation, Sam found that each door and window had an oak leaf lightly resting on the handle. So it seemed, the ghost was gone and with it, the pursuing wind. But the days of peace and quiet were short lived. On the roads and woods surrounding the  the house, stories of freak storms, ghostly riders and unearthly howls began to surface in the local media. The rumors continued to grow, spreading in conversations in the bars over beer mugs and across shopping carts at the grocery store. The spirit, forced away from the house by the Hunt, had run free. Run, apparently, towards Chatham.

Sam was reluctant to discuss this with the others, but they came to the same conclusion. The Hunt too had moved on and was now racketing about the Cape. A series of deadly snow and ice storms, unusual for the Cape and the time of the year, made November a grim struggle. Sudden fogs surrounded drivers on the roads and  hikers and runners in the woods, causing them to lose their bearings completely. In the eerie murk, strange voices and howls and muffled hoofbeats were heard. Downed power lines, blocked roads and heavy storm surges endangered human lives and the fragile world of the ocean borderlands. As the reports of increasingly destructive sightings came trickling in, the residents of the Inn realized that something needed to be done.

It was completely by chance that they found the folklorist. That Saturday afternoon Sam was tidying up the dining room after a busy brunch. As she pottered around with place settings for the evening meal, Harry Barbieri struck up a conversation with her. Harry was a long-time Cape resident, red-faced, jovial, and after the five mimosas he had consumed during brunch, overflowing with goodwill towards humanity. It was the perfect opportunity to indulge in his favorite pastime of spreading light and joy in the life of those nearest to him, preferably those of the female persuasion. Conversation shifted from the excellence of the brunch to life in the Midwest and New York city, when Sam disclosed that in her previous life she had been an anthropology professor. Harry's conversation dried up abruptly, and his face began to take on that furtive, hangdog look people acquire on discovering they are talking to a teacher or a policeman. "Anthropology?" he said, "that's cool. Very cool." After an awkward silence, during which he fidgeted with and rearranged Sam's place settings incorrectly, he offered, "Then you ought to meet the folklorist, right! You would have a lot to talk about."

All of Sam's tiredness vanished. "The folklorist?" she said sharply, fixing him with an intense look, "What folklorist?"

Being the focus of the full attention of a self-confessed ex-professor made Harry distinctly nervous. Beginning to edge away, he said, "Don't you know, it's the guy who lives out in the marshes. Old Evan. Knocked around all over the world and then settled here with that library of his. Strange fellow! You should get along fine!" As the implications of his last remark sank in, too late, he became completely tongue-tied. Luckily, his wife came in just then, brandishing the recipe for Phil's bouillabaisse, and bore him away, promising to return the next week.


Eileen and Dori, on being questioned, were forced to admit they did not know of the folklorist. But Dori's cousin Gracie, who lived out in the wilds of Eastham, did. So it happened that three days later, Sam, Beth and Phil found themselves seated in a small cottage on the edge of the salt marsh at Nauset. There was a fire in the hearth, two overfed cats, and bookcases lining the walls of the living room. The books overflowed on to the floor where they were stacked knee high along the walls. The hallway was similarly occupied, as were the stairs and the dining room  glimpsed as they entered.

They were hospitably welcomed and made comfortable, with beakers of single malt to fuel the conversation.

In appearance and manner the folklorist resembled Sherlock Holmes. "Or rather, like Jeremy Brett playing Sherlock Holmes," thought Sam, drifting into a pleasant daydream, lulled by the warmth of the fire, the comfort of the chair, and the droning voice of the folklorist as he discoursed on mythology. A vision of domestic bliss unfolded before her inner eye - the small cottage, with climbing roses, cats, the fireplace, Sherlock's pipe, the ashes he scattered everywhere, his habit of practicing marksmanship indoors and the resulting mess of plaster and dust. No, it would not Do. Despite his brilliance, Holmes was a domestic Menace.

She returned with a start to the present and found the Folklorist in the middle of an exposition of early European pagan beliefs: "....varied across each of the geographical locations in which the tradition was found. But the basic idea was generally the same - a phantasmal leader, accompanied by a horde of hounds and men, hurtled through the night sky, their passing marked by a tumultuous racket of pounding hooves, howling dogs and raging winds. In England the riders were known as the Gabriel Hounds, in Teutonic myth as Odin's Ride and in Celtic lands as...."
"The Wild Hunt," Sam said, heedlessly interrupting.

Three pairs of eyes looked at her, questioning. "They were here," she continued awkwardly "the night of the storm. I saw them."

All three spoke together: "Where?" "You saw them?" "Not at the inn? Oh please, not near my inn?"

"I didn't actually see," she said, embarrassed now, "I heard them, actually. But I knew that's what they must be."

"You mean, the wind that hounds the spook is the Wild Hunt?" Phil said slowly.

"But that's impossible," said Beth, "it's just a story. They're not real! It's only a myth."

The folklorist turned his austere gaze on her. "And what, exactly, is a myth except a way of making sense of reality, when that reality does not make sense?"

Phil was an avid public television watcher. "So myth is a way of making the world," he said.

"Exactly," said the folklorist, approvingly "of making and remaking. And that is the key. You must remake this story."

For a long time he was silent, gazing into the fire. Finally he spoke, reluctantly but with authority: "You must summon the Hunt."

For a moment they were too shocked to speak. Phil tried, gamely, to take it in his stride: "Summon the Hunt! Just like that? What do we do, mail them an invitation? Or can we find them on Facebook?"

The folklorist frowned: "This is no laughing matter. Indeed, you may never in your lives face such danger again. But the signs are clear and your story confirms it. The lines are beginning to blur, and great evil may ride free unless this spirit can be stopped. Only the Hunter can tell you how."

He rose and walked over the fire to shift the glowing logs. They took this to mean that the audience was over.

"I must think upon this," he said in farewell, "prepare yourselves for a fateful meeting."

# 7. The paths that cross

News of the ghost spread rapidly and the Inn, located conveniently close to the sightings, was besieged by journalists. Beth hired six new servers to work two shifts everyday, persuaded them to cover their tattoos. The living room was perforce converted into a lounge and makeshift bar, and was soon overrun with journalists thrilled to be in at the scene of the hauntings. The new helpers were a mixed bunch. There was Gabriella, an older Salvadorian woman who was glad to find work in the off season. There were Steve and Jim, students at the culinary institute who dove out from Medford ninety miles each way, as work was hard to come by. Bill was a DJ. Kathy cleaned houses, designed cartoon frogs and sang karaoke at the VFW on Friday nights dressed as a pirate.

The conversations in the dining room were idiosyncratically and uniquely Cape. Passing through the crowded room with a tray loaded with cocktails Sam overheard enigmatic snatches:

"This morning I was going to throw myself under a bus but then I didn't."

"Oh well, it's the thought that counts."

In the middle of this unexpected rush, the folklorist showed up unannounced.

Fortunately, it was a Monday evening, and football took precedence over ghost hunting.

Due to Beth's firm refusal to allow any size of television screen in areas devoted to food and drink, the bar and dining room were deserted. It was Daisy who discovered Old Evan pottering around outside the house. Normally a placid dog, she set up a frantic barking, scratching at the kitchen door and demanding to be let out. Sam nervously made up her mind to go out and confront possible intruders lurking in the twilight. The moment she opened the door, Daisy streaked out and headed for the old stricken oak.

Sam, following some way behind, came upon the unforgettable sight of the folklorist, his dignity intact, lying flat on his back while Daisy stood over him with front paws on his chest, wagging her tail furiously. Once he had been rescued and restored to an upright position, he began to examine the tree and the paths running up to it closely.

"Ha! Yes, I see. Most remarkable," he exclaimed, as he wandered from tree to tree, "they do cross. As I feared..."

"You feared? It sounds like you would expect to find spirits here!?"

"Well of course, it stands to reason that this is where they would gather. It's the lines, you see, ley lines, the lines of power. This is where they cross."

And indeed, watching him make little darts, first in one direction and then another, Sam suddenly had a clear vision of two crossing paths right there by the tree. There was the one that came up the little gully, with the running path leading to, or away from, the state forest where the hawks nest; it crossed the path that picked up where the road to

Seawind ended.


Returning to the clearing by the tree, and keeping a wary eye on Daisy, Evan addressed

the questions crowding into Sam's mind, though she hadn't spoken. Attaching his

hands to his coat lapels in a lecturing pose he began: "They're spirit paths, or faery

paths. And when these roads meet and cross, they make a place of great power. There's

one right near here, just where the woods begin, by the oak tree."

"But I thought ley lines were good things," said Sam, "not that I know anything about

them."

"They're not good or bad in themselves," he replied, half his words lost as he turned

away, now sniffing the branches at nose level, "They're just power, which can be used

for good or evil." Sam was silent but her thoughts persisted like an eight-year old child

facing an unknowable mystery. "But why here? Why this house, this time, this place?"


These were the paths she took when she went running in the afternoons. It was difficult

to see these peaceful, everyday surroundings as the mythic ley lines. They felt right of

course, following the natural contours of the land. Built to a human scale, by

generations of people following animal paths, not designed by corps of engineers. But

perhaps not only human. The crossroads, Evan said, drew the evil spirit and the Hunt that pursued him. And they had, also, unwittingly, offered it an escape from the paths

set by the Hunt, so it could run free and destroy the world.

"The crossroads, and the tracks themselves are crossing places. Water is a boundary and

a portal. Certain days and times...twilight, the change of the seasons...."

"lHalloween," Sam picked up the thought, "yes, that just might make sense. That was

the day I first heard the Hunt....And the ghost, though I didn't know what it was."

"Just so," said the folklorist, and turned back to his examination of the clearing and its

terrain. The Sherlockian effect of his appearance was heightened by his odd movements

and exclamations as he lay down full length with his ear to the ground. Sam thought of

offering him a tarpaulin to spread on the ground, but he didn't seem to mind the pine

needles and leaf mould accumulating on his clothes.


"I have never thought of this as an evil place," she mused aloud.

"The power in itself is not good or evil, but can be turned to any purpose," he

explained, "an evil spirit could tap into the lines, as it were, to bring about great

destruction. As seems to be happening indeed."

They were silent for a long time, until Daisy began to nudge them hopefully in the

direction of the kitchen door. Seemingly oblivious of the cold, Evan continued to ponder

the discovery of the paths: "They offer a portal to the spirit to enter the world, and to

escape into the paths into the wide world. But, they are also the lines of fate, and it may well be that the spirit came here to meet its fate. This may be the place where the Hunt will run its quarry to earth, after it makes amends for its wrongdoing....."

But it was when they finally went indoors for a hot drink that Evan made his major discovery. Sebastian trotted busily into the room, and jumped gracefully up to the window sill. His presence electrified the folklorist.

"Now this might explain a great deal," he said, eyeing Sebastian with a mixture of respect and curiosity, "did you know that black cats were considered lucky by sailors? And that sailors' families always had one as a pet? In Scarborough, others were unable to find or keep a black cat, they were so much in demand by the sailors."

Sebastian said, "Mee-yuff" in gracious benediction, as if in thanks for his understanding of the Importance of Cats. Sam knew from experience that this was his way of saying, "I told you so."

"Now cats," continued Evan, addressing himself more to Sebastian than his human audience, "cats know all about the lines of power and they love them. It's like walking the tightrope for them. They can handle the power and control it."

Sebastian soon tired of his new admirer, and dozed off perched precariously on the back of the sofa and in danger of sliding down behind the cushions. To improve matters he soon turned himself upside down and continued napping with all four paws in the air. Luckily for the hospitality of the house, the humans took a greater interest in the folklorist's rambling discourse and gradually detached themselves from their chores to join in his audience.

Evan mused on his odd career, which he had spent collecting tales of hauntings and faery paths in Celtic lands. "It began, of course, with a college course in anthropology," he said, with an apologetic look at Sam. She suppressed a sigh. She had heard that before. At times she felt that there should be a minimum age for an introduction to anthropology, as there was for alcohol. Or that anthropology course descriptions should contain a statutory warning, similar those used for addictive substances. Nevertheless, despite the concentrated brilliance and eccentricity of the discipline, Evan continued, there was something missing. Perhaps ironically for a field which could claim *The Golden Bough* as a foundational text, anthropology in all its branches had thrown its lot with the humanistic and scientific vision of modernity, turning its back on the mysteries that were inseparable from life and existence. After Cambridge, his journeys had taken Evan to some odd corners of the world, including the conflict zones of Northern Ireland, Palestine, Cyprus, and the Congo. There were no answers anywhere, no clues. He borrowed the words of the Great Detective himself: "What is the meaning of it? What is the object of this circle of misery and violence and fear? It must have a purpose, or our universe has no meaning and that is unthinkable. But what purpose? That is humanity's great problem, for which reason so far has no answer."

If anything, myth with its dramatization of the conflict of good and evil, gave a hint of understanding the chaos of existence. After two decades of knocking around the world, collecting myths and working in refugee camps, he decided to settle down. A chance visit to a cousin vacationing on the Cape brought him to Nauset and the salt marshes, which felt like home. He decided to sell his house in the Home Counties, which had never been anything more than a base from which to conduct his travels. His immense library was transplanted, too, and he joined the ranks of Cape Cod eccentrics, who found a refuge in its very remoteness.

"Strange to live in a place of such beauty to meditate on the madness and cruelty of humankind, I suppose," he concluded, "but that may be the reason why it works."

He had written a series of books on myth and violence that had become runaway bestsellers, and consequently spent much time fending off pressing invitations from New Age groups, medievalists and folklore societies to participate their events. He guarded his privacy fiercely and his presence at *Seawind* was a testament to the seriousness of the danger posed by a spirit that could evade the Hunt.


The next week, Sam drove down to New York for a long-overdue meeting and lunch with her editor. She regarded it as an interruption of her search for the meaning of the Hunt, but as it turned out, the same conversation continued with a different location and personae. She had learnt the hard way not to drive all the way into the city, having spent hours getting into Manhattan by way of one of the bottlenecks, euphemistically called bridges. She parked in New Haven and took the commuter train to Grand Central, reliving with the journey flashbacks to the number of times she had traveled that route, which seemed several lifetimes ago.

The city was humming with energy as usual. Despite her ambivalent love-hate relationship with the place where she had spent some of the most difficult and productive years of her life, it was impossible not to get caught up in its pace and beat. Just being there gave her a major caffeine buzz that lasted the whole day and well into the night. She had persuaded Max to meet her in Chinatown rather than one of the terminally cool wine bars in Soho or Dumbo that were his natural habitat. Max Whittington was a bright young thirty-something who had founded the coolest (or hottest, Sam wasn't sure which) new literary magazine of the decade, combining progressive politics with exquisite writing and gut-wrenching analysis. He was good-looking, intelligent, compassionate and utterly devoted to Sam. She couldn't help wishing he was fifteen years older. So now they were safely ensconced at a table in a tiny Vietnamese restaurant, one of her old haunts. Time seemed to pass it by: the fatherly waiters, the crisp shrimp rolls with lettuce, the tall glasses of iced coffee, and the cheerful lunchtime crowd were all exactly as she remembered them.

Max, she discovered, had gone from his prep school Latin days to become something of

an expert on European myth. He was very interested in all she had to tell him about the

visit to the folklorist and the Wild Hunt.

"They are indeed the messengers of death," he commented, expertly mixing his iced

coffee as he focused his thoughts and words, "and as such, fearsome. But also essential,

and in some senses, part of the natural and moral universe. You only have to think of

the Vedic Yamaduta and the Greeks' Charon, who conducted souls to the kingdom of

the dead, to understand your own reaction to the Wild Hunt. Are you going to eat

that?" He ended on an agitated note, as Sam squirted an enormous helping of chili

sauce in her bowl of noodle soup.

She carried on mixing in the chili sauce, intent only on solving the mystery of the Hunt:

"Hm, that would explain why having an evil spirit elude the Hunt could throw the

universe out of  whack?" She had missed spices and spicy foods on the Cape. "Is that

how the dots connect up? Ghost and Hunt? What is the Hunt? Why is it here?"

"Didn't you say there was a different feel to the Hunt? Fey but not evil?"

"And the ghost, by contrast feels evil. Which brings me back to my original question:

What is the Hunt?"

"There are all kinds of twists and turns to the pattern, of course," said Max, casting

doubtful glances at Sam's lunch, and the bright red which was now the predominant color in her bowl, "the Wild Hunt, for example, fearsome as it is, only goes after true evil. And it has its redeeming features, too."

"Redeeming features? Let me guess," she said, "they give candy to kids and help little old ladies across the street in their spare time from scaring the citizenry half to death?"

"You need to watch those spices, they make you cranky," Max was unperturbed, "but really, though the Hunt is fearsome and even mortally dangerous to behold, it hunts and harries only the evil that not does not belong, and will not leave."

"Evil does not belong," mused Sam, "but does it?"

"The eternal question, or one them, isn't it?" said Max, "but maybe the pagans had it right. Can there be good without evil, beauty without arousing envy and hatred? Or is their existence part of the natural order of things?"


"Well, I'm glad to hear that you don't think of the Hunt as evil," said Sam "that's not the feeling I get from them, unlike the ghost."

"You and your friends may even be glad to learn that the Hunt is said to bring good luck to those it visits, leaving gifts of silver."

Sam was indeed glad to hear that there was something to look forward to.

# 8. The Search

Now that Beth had new kitchen helpers, Sam had the time to put her research into the house and family's past on a serious footing. The first step was to find out more about the *Seawind,* the ship that bore the same name as the house. She discovered by doing an online search for Cape Cod shipwrecks that the records of the Boston Seaman's Friend Society were kept at the Congregational Library on Beacon Street in Boston. The newsletters and bulletins dated back to 1827. On a cold grey day in the middle of November she drove the eighty miles down to Boston. Looking for parking in the rain and then paying a small fortune - after first having to find an ATM, since the parking lot didn't accept credit cards - did nothing to lift her spirits. After having lived in New York for fifteen years, she found Bostonians almost excessively polite. But only on foot. Once ensconced behind the steering wheels of their cars, they turned into maniacs. In either case, the contrast with New York was sobering and instructive. She trudged wearily down the street, the monumental architecture lost on her, reflecting uncharitably on Boston's deep connection to its Puritan heritage.

Libraries were her natural habitat, however, and the rituals of consultation with the reference desk, searching the stacks with her neck at an odd angle with a small slip of paper clutched in her hand, discovering the right volumes and settling down at the enormous oaken table restored her equanimity and curiosity. The March 1882 issue of the Society's bulletin carried the news of the sinking of the clipper *Seawind.* Sailing out of Boston for the West Indies, the ship ran aground at Chatham during a storm, and was lost. All forty crew and six officers perished. The news item had the information Sam was looking for: the captain of the unfortunate ship was Edward Cartwright of West Chatham, Massachusetts. The ship's owner was listed as William Barnaby, of Boston.

Caught up in her search, Sam began methodically searching through the bulletins for any more news of the unfortunate ship. She struck lucky a second time. Amid the hirsute splendor of nineteenth century ministers, educators, reformers and captains of industry, one clean-shaven face stood out sharply. Long dark hair, sweeping eyebrows, piercing eyes. Sam had found the ghost. William Barnaby had been a prominent banker, shipowner and financier. And murderer, Sam added to herself, remembering her vivid dream. She sat for a long time in the reading room with its high ceilings and gold-edged friezes, staring blindly out into the grey rain. The worlds were not separate after all. Here at last were the connections between ghost, dream and the family at *Seawind.* The connections between past and present, magic and the everyday, were not after all safely contained in fiction, a escape from what she thought was the real world. She had never taken seriously the notion that such these tales might contain some germ of the truth, or that she might herself encounter that truth some day. And yet all her experience and instincts told her that before her on the oaken desk lay proof that the spirits and dreams

were rooted in a real crime, one that happened a hundred and forty years ago.


Driving back to the Cape always gave her a strange feeling of going home. As the air

became clearer and the landscape empty of signs of human habitation, the self-

contained world of the Cape drew her into its own magic. And yet, she reflected even

Eden had its serpent. There was something about unearthly beauty that attracted

unearthly evil. Enchantment works both ways.


As she turned off the highway, the temperature dropped sharply and the clouds that

had been murking the sky all day suddenly opened up with freezing hailstones. A fierce

wind rocked the car and she had to fight to hold the steering steady. She could see other

cars weaving across the road as they were seized by the wind and the drivers lost

control. The traffic lights swung wildly and stopped functioning. As she neared the turn

on Route 28, the street lights went out. Luckily it was not far to *Seawind* and she made it

back safely, without any mishaps. Others were not so fortunate and that evening's news

was full of crashes and accidents, related by grim-faced anchors and officials.


The hailstorm had been followed by sleet and icy rain. The ice storm held the Cape in

its grip for two whole days, during which the roads were impassable and howling winds added to the discomfort caused by downed power lines. The fury of the storm seemed to be concentrated around Chatham, at the corner where the Cape turned northwards. Evan was convinced that the fierce struggle between the ghost and the Hunt had moved out to the Sands.

Sam's discovery of  the ghost's identity confirmed the belief that he was not a native of the Cape. It also sent Phil off on a search for William Barnaby. He took to spending hours at the public libraries and historical societies, searching for any mention of the shipowner. It took him a week to find what he was looking for, and then it was not in the historical records, but a popular book on pirates and witches.

"Will Barnaby had a local reputation as a financier and crook, a witch, with a particular power to call up storms at sea." he announced that evening after dinner as they met in the morning room to compare notes.

"A dubious skill for a shipowner," said Beth, whose skepticism had not been shaken by the manifestations and the wreckage caused by the freak hailstorm in downtown Chatham, which featured prominently in the TV news and *The Cape Cod Times*. She persisted in attributing them to extremely localized bad weather events.

"It echoed the story of the witch of Eastham, who back in 1771 was said to have called up a storm at sea to sink the pirate ship Wyddah ....." Phil continued undaunted.

"Why would he need to call up a storm? If their weather was anything like what we're

having, there would be plenty of storms anyway."

"Ah, but there is a point. To call up a storm at a particular time and place, to sink a

particular ship."

"The *Seawind*?"

"Exactly!"

"But isn't he listed as the shipowner? Why would he sink his own ship?"

Beth didn't see that as a puzzle at all. She assumed that a banker, even a nineteenth

century one, would have no compunction about destroying lives and property to serve

his own ends. And she may have been right. It remained however to be discovered

what those ends were.

According to Phil's book, those who knew William Barnaby or had any dealings with

him quickly recognized that his character was founded on malice and betrayal. It was

rumored that he had defrauded widows and orphans of sailors lost at sea of their

rightful inheritance. Not content with that, he had embezzled funds from the Seaman's

Friend Society. No one dared to accuse him out loud, but at the time of his death, the

whispers were getting louder and louder.


"But listen to this," Phil was still turning the pages of his book, "he came to a bad end.

As you will doubtless be glad to learn. It says that in the last months of his life he seemed to have taken leave  of his senses and was often seen wandering around

Chatham sands muttering to himself, heedless of weather and tides, at all hours of day

and night. And one night, the tide took him."

"So he didn't really benefit from his crimes," said Beth.

"No, but he caused a lot of suffering all the same," Sam was remembering the dream in

which she had seen William Barnaby bludgeon an injured man to death. "Not to

mention that he was probably a murderer as well, even if his crime went undetected."

As Beth and Phil looked at her uncomprehendingly, Sam realized that there was one

piece of the story they did not know. She described her vivid dream and there was a

long silence when she had finished.

Finally Beth said, "That makes perfect sense, when you think about the aura of evil he

carries around with him." She was no longer a sceptic.

# 9. The Summoning

Thanksgiving was a subdued affair on the Cape. Perhaps because here better than anywhere else, the ugly truth behind the myth was widely known. Indeed Cape residents went out of their way to set the record straight, using any occasion and forum whether suitable or not to announce that the gift of corn was in fact a theft, stolen by the colonists from the Indians' winter store. Facing the prospect of starvation, the Indians attempted to recover their stores. The resulting skirmish left five of them dead. And it went downhill from there.

As winter approached, the storms became worse and worse. That weekend saw the worst winter weather recorded in over eighty years, as a howling nor'easter dumped six feet of snow, felled trees, froze traffic lights and cut power lines across New England. Hundreds of thousands of people were left without heating and light for weeks, as restoring power was a slow tedious process. Libraries and cafes became places of refuge, from homes that had no heat and no running water.

Strange new crimes surfaced. On beaches from Chatham to Dennis, seals were being murdered, mysteriously bludgeoned to death. Police investigations led absolutely nowhere. It seemed that there was a violent, evil spirit at large, bent upon destruction. It was the seal deaths that moved the folklorist to action. On the day the eighth murder was reported, he called Sam.

"The moon is full tonight," he said, "we must be ready."

It was a spell of four, he explained. It needed four people to cast and hold such wild spirits as the Hunt. They were to meet just before midnight near the inn, at the oak tree that had been struck by lightning. It was already afternoon. The days were drawing in early, and it was dark by four o'clock. Sam and Beth went about their tasks weighed by a mixture of feelings in which anticipation and dread predominated. It was like going to the dentist to have a tooth pulled out. Phil was distracted too, switching at random between books on cookery and mythology as he feverishly chopped, sautéed and simmered while muttering to himself. This unlikely method produced a masterpiece of a casserole for dinner.

By nine o'clock their nerves were on edge and the wind had risen to a howling gale. The folklorist had warned them against alcohol, so they drank coffee instead. The animals were huddled in the attic. At eleven Sam's cell phone chimed out the opening bars of "People are strange". It was Evan, and he was stranded. A heavy tree branch, felled by the wind, was blocking the road leading from his house to Route 6, and no crews could get to it at night.

"...walk to the nearest.....a mile away," Sam heard. His voice came erratically over the phone. They could barely hear each other. For a moment his voice cut in strong and clear: "I have found the verse that summons the Hunt on a night of the Full Moon, but wait for me! Only four together can hold! Four is the magic number! You must all learn the Summoning.

By the Lines that Cross

By the Light of the Moon

By the weathered Oak,

We command: Stand and Speak!"

His voice vanished and was replaced by static and finally silence. Sam hung up, and turned to the others. "He says to wait for him," she said, "We must be four to summon. It's too dangerous to try without him."

"It's too dangerous NOT to try," said Beth, "Every day the ghost gets wilder."

"Well, if we must, we must," said Phil, "Now which tree is it?"


Under the oak, its leafless branches casting clear shadows in the full light of the moon, they held hands to form a circle and spoke the words of summoning, then waited for the Hunt. And it came. First, a far-off neighing and a jingle of harness bells, and then faster than thought, hoofbeats shaking the ground, they were there, horses rearing, capes flying, and at their head, the Hunter himself. They stopped a bare ten feet away from the three humans standing motionless as if they too had been spelled. The Hunt turned and chafed in fruitless efforts to free itself from the summons. The horses reared and tossed their heads, hounds with eyes of fire lunged and bayed, but the spell held them.

Close up, the Hunt was the stuff of primal nightmares. Vaguely human in form and appearance, they were utterly alien and fey in feeling. The brilliant moonlight produced an answering cold gleam from axes and jagged sword blades, harness and bells attached to the hunting birds' trailing jesses. At the head of the Hunt was Herne himself, Cernunnos the antler-headed god. His rage at being summoned and held created an aura which outlined the whole company in red and green flame, battling with the silver moonlight. A bird of prey on his wrist screamed and spread its wings, its eyes and sharp curving beak gleaming red and silver.

Nor were the summoners free. They stood rooted in fear, feet unable to follow the instinct to flee, while their minds stove to break the chains of physical existence, to be somewhere this Fear was not. The leader of the Hunt spoke in a voice like thunder: "Mortals, Dare you summon the Hunt!" A long frozen moment passed. The silence angered him further. He spoke again, this time mockingly "Such craven beings to summon the spirits of the wind! Speak, thou!"

Sam's voice came out as a squeak, "It's about that ghost...um, spirit, that you're

hunting."

Her mouth was dry and her tongue seemed glued to the roof of her mouth, but she

struggled to speak: "He doesn't belong here, you see. And in fact, neither do you."

The Hunter turned his full face to her. Only the spell kept her from burrowing beneath

the carpet of dry leaves at her feet. His voice was the roar of thunder, the whiplash of

lightening: "We seek that which is our right. All evil must be hunted, that is the law."

Beth was standing outside his line of vision. With a great effort, she spoke, "Um, you

see, that's it exactly. You don't seem to be succeeding. And it's destroying the Cape."

Face to face with The Lord of the Hunt, Phil continued to be his frank, helpful,

Midwestern self: "In fact, we think you're lost. You've gone off the tracks. And your

quarry keeps escaping you."


Cheerful honesty was definitely the wrong tone. It was not appreciated by the spectral

horde, already enraged by their failure and the summoning. The spell would not hold

the Hunt, the numbers were wrong. They should have listened to Old Evan. If anything

could be more fearful than the Hunt itself, it was the Hunt's anger. The Hunter raised

his arm, in his hand a long spear flashed sparks of red fire. The spell frayed and as the

horses leapt forward, Phil stumbled forward to shield the other two. The spear caught him in the middle, flashed right through his body and vanished. He fell to the ground. The Hunt moved forward again, and gathering speed, rode over him as the others watched in horror. Then it was gone, leaving behind only the moon caught in the branches of the oak, as in a cage. They ran to Phil, and helped him as he tried to sit up. Miraculously, there was no blood and no visible marks of injury. But in the moonlight they could see that his eyes were unfocused, and he shivered without stopping. He couldn't speak and could barely hold his head up.

As they struggled up the path to the carriage house, Daisy burst out of the house, closely followed by Eileen and Dori. Sebastian brought up the rear of this procession, trying to look nonchalant, as if he just happened to find himself in their company. There was no doubt about their purpose, though. They formed a ring around Phil and escorted him, now able to stand upright and walk in a kind of stagger, to the living room couch. Sebastian and Daisy took up their positions at his head and feet respectively, while the two old ladies went into a huddled conversation from which a few grim words reached Beth and Sam. Fey, sickness, iron and silver were whispered back and forth. Then the indomitable duo of retirees marched into the tiny galley kitchen and in quick succession produced drinks of hot water, the first with an iron key, then a silver ring at the bottom of the cup. Phil drank them unresisting and fell into an uneasy, shivery sleep, with both animals huddled close as if they were his bodyguard.

Old Evan stopped by the day after the failed summoning to ask after Phil. But he mortally offended Beth by being unsuitably amused by the mishaps of the evening. In fact, he laughed till the tears ran down his seamed cheeks.

"The spectral Keystone Cops, no less," he sputtered, "well, that's definitely one for the books!" As Beth's ominous silence persisted, he sobered up a little.

"Not too many mortals have survived an encounter with the Hunt," he said, "so you may consider yourselves fortunate. But should this become known, be prepared for hordes of folklorists and medievalists to descend upon you to chronicle the event. That horror is nearly on par with meeting the Hunt itself."

As he contemplated the event, he broke into more guffaws and gasps of laughter, and they could get no more sense out of him, for that afternoon at least. The one helpful thing he said was to remind them of the different feel to the Hunt. Fey but not evil, as Sam remembered; that, probably, was the reason for Phil's miraculous escape.

It was three days before Phil was well enough to walk into kitchen, almost fully recovered except for a slight shaking of the hands when he tired. By a process of trial and error they had discovered that a diet of lemonade and tuna salad on crusty sourdough bread seemed to help him. After the first dose, he refused to drink any more of Dori's iron-tempered water, but it had already done its work removing the fey sickness. His illness and recovery had been accompanied by marvelous dreams, which eluded him on waking. All he remembered was that they involved cooking, in the best equipped kitchens he had ever seen. And there was no washing up at the end. To Beth's annoyance, he was rather reluctant to leave his sickbed to return to the inn's kitchen and the task of feeding the hordes of journalists.

But when he did return to the kitchen, it was as something of a triumph. Always an inspired cook, his dinners were now being described as out of this world, and began attracting a new breed of journalist. Not only the stormchasers and garrulous ghost hunters, but odd figures from the gourmet beat began dropping by at mealtimes. But it was a retired sportscaster, once famous for his football commentaries, who made the real breakthrough. After a meal during which he consumed food and drink in alarming quantities, he stopped dead at his first bite of lemon soufflé. Then he  pulled out his cellphone and carefully dialed a number, which turned out to be his producer. With drunken dignity, he explained to the VIP - Very Important Producer - at the other end of the line that he had discovered culinary heaven, and that the network should send someone down to tie up a deal for a series, before rival stations arrived. He then handed over the phone to Phil and returned to his dessert.

Phil went into a huddle with the phone near the windows, where the reception was a little better, and after fifteen minutes, came back to the kitchen looking thoughtful and twitchy.

"That was John Starr," he said, "he's one of the biggest names in television. And he wants to come here. And bring his food correspondent."

As the kitchen, full of helpers and hangers-on, exploded into cheers and back-slapping, Phil continued to look thoughtful, rubbing the two-day stubble he had cultivated since the encounter with the Hunt.

"Did you say they weren't actually evil?" he asked Sam.

"Well, it was my editor, actually," she replied, "fearsome but not evil, is what he thought."

"I wonder," he said, and stopped.

"Gifts..." he tried again, "did he say something about gifts?"

"He did, at that," said Sam, and they left the matter there for the moment.

# 10. Voices in the air

Meanwhile Sam turned the basement upside down in her search for any more information on the family's history. There was no sort of order to the accumulated junk of seven or more generations stored there, and she began working her way from front to back through the fascinating hoard that filled the trunks, boxes, chests of drawers and armoires. Clothes, jewelry, china ornaments, gloves, hats, dinnerware, linens, books, journals - someday, they would make a wonderful archive. For her present purposes, they represented nothing more than distractions for Sam. She had to keep a tight rein on her imagination and an eye on the clock as she worked. One wooden crate full of journals seemed promising, but turned out to contain a series of sketchbooks, with exquisite, detailed pictures of seaside and marsh grasses, weeds, flowers, mosses, stones and algae. Sam spent two happy and fruitless hours browsing through these before admitting that they could not have anything useful to tell her about the house and its haunting.

She finally found what she was looking for in a cedar hope chest, in remarkably good shape despite its great age. Within a nest of fine linens lay a battered blue-bound book. It was a journal, bound in pale blue leather with a design of gold flowers and leaves running around the edges. The humidity of the climate had warped and twisted the leather binding. The once-rich cream paper was worn at the edges and stained. Opening it cautiously, Sam found faded brown writing, a childish cursive. And  the date she was looking for: 1882. Carrying it upstairs in triumph, she found that the others had no time to spare for it. Beth had her hands full, following Phil's cooking directions as he feverishly tried to recreate the recipes from his dreams for the pilot show.  Sam took the blue-bound book away to her attic bedroom to read.

Despite its battered condition, it had clearly once been a beautiful and prized object, suitable for a young girl's keepsake journal. Following her bad habit of reading the end of detective novels first, Sam turned to the last pages. She justified this practice to herself by arguing that knowing the identity of the killer didn't spoil the book, but enabled her to appreciate the psychological and plot twists all the more. In this case, however, she wished she had never read those entries. The writing ended only about a third of the way into the journal. The last entry was date February 16, 1882. That would make it exactly one week after the sinking of *Seawind* and the murder of Edward Cartwright.

*"This is the last time I will write my journal. In one week I have lost my father and my home.*

*We are to go away and live with Mama's relatives in Quincy. They do not care for pets, so my*

*dear Storm kitty has been given away. Her new home has kind people, but I know she will miss*

Sam was used, in the course of her work, to reading and hearing about political violence from those who had survived it. She was familiar with the depths to which the human soul could sink, and the courage with which survivors continued their lives. Reading a journal of misfortune written by a sixteen-year old girl a century and a half ago, in the very room it was written, was an  experience of a different order. The contrast with the happy beginning of the journal was almost unbearable. Six months earlier, it had begun with cheerful faith in their homecoming.



Marie had claimed the attic rooms for her own, had lived and slept and dreamt in the same rooms that Sam herself now shared with Sebastian. Much of the journal was full of the events and life of a sixteen-year old - lessons, visits to the beach, picnics with friends and their families, church and Sunday school. Yet there were hints already of a threat that could not be concealed, even from the children.

*"Yesterday Mr. Barnaby came to visit my father again and they were closeted in the book room for over an hour. We could hear shouting, and after he left my father locked the doors very carefully. This morning mother took me aside and told me the whole, 'For you are not a child any longer.' It seems that Mr. Barnaby had lent my father the money to buy our beloved home, and now, instead of waiting for it to be repaid over time as originally agreed, he wants it all right now. 'But what shall we do?' I cried, 'are we to leave our house and become homeless beggars? What will become of Storm-kitty and the horses?' But my mother said to have faith in father's ability and courage. For he was planning another voyage, to the East this time, to trade for goods that would fetch a fabulous price in the cities of Boston and New York."*

Barnaby, it seemed, was pressing Edward to return the money he had lent for the house. The details weren't clear, but there were rumors that Barnaby had been cheating his partners in Boston and they were threatening him with public disgrace and prison. He in turn called in his loans, regardless of the original agreements. In order to find the money to repay him for the house, Edward Cartwright decided to revisit the east, where he had travelled before. He was confident that he could bring back goods that would be worth a fortune. But first he was forced to pledge his ship for a sum of money that he needed to carry with him. William Barnaby managed, through a whispering campaign

that cast doubts on the *Seawind's* soundness, to turn all the Boston financiers against the

journey. In the end Edward was forced to turn to none other than Barnaby himself. With

his home and his ship pledged to his bitterest enemy, Edward Cartwright set sail in the

*Seawind* for the ancient land of Persia.


Yet in the beginning the journey went well, and Edward wrote home of his success.

*"We have had a letter today! All about it is strange, the postmark, the writings, the very paper it*

*is written on. It comes from the land where my father travels, and he has good news for us. He*

*has journeyed long and far in a strange but hospitable place. And at last, he has found that which*

*he was looking for, in the shop of a merchant in the city of Isphahan. He writes  of rugs and*

*fabrics of a richness never seen in our commonwealth, and of jewels fit for a queen. Above all he*

*writes of a necklace and bracelets of Persian gold, with pendants shaped like roses. These, he says,*

*he will not sell but bring home for my mother and myself."*

Sam knew the bitter ending of that journey, for she had witnessed it herself, in her

dream.

————


Halfway into December, the freak storms began. Centered on Chatham, where the land

turned sharp left and north, they blew up out of nowhere, invisible on radar until the raging winds had the land in their icy grip. There was something unnatural about the blizzards. Residents began to imagine voices in the winds, unearthly howls, hoofbeats, dogs barking. The Hunt had broken free of the lines of power in pursuit of the spirit of Barnaby, who now haunted the Chatham sands after being closed out of the house. Beaches were eaten away even in the comparatively quieter waters of the Sound. Houses on the cliff edges considered safe were suddenly in danger of falling down as wind and wild water tore away the land from beneath them. Snow and ice covered the northeast. Parts of the sound began to freeze over, trapping small fishing boats. Coast guard cutters had to double as icebreakers and escorts for the fishing fleets.

Violent storms with whiteout conditions sprang up unexpectedly all over the north-east, but reserved a special fury for Chatham. TV crews and national broadcasters from Boston and New York descended upon the outer Cape in a flurry of self-importance but the long drive out sobered them up. Equipped with the latest storm tracking equipment and extreme weather gear, they nevertheless found themselves dealing with something primal and unknowable. Their fear and discomfort showed clearly on their faces. Reporters who had broadcast in the face of hurricanes in Florida and twisters in the Midwest were visibly spooked on TV, their words vague, their eyes wandering skyward, as they heard echoes of the  Hunt all around them in the air. Even the TV microphones picked up the thunder of hoofs and screaming horses. Sam fancied she could even hear Barnaby's howls of rage and despair, as background to the nervy chatter of the reporters.

Between storms, dense fog blanketed the coastal areas for days on end, all the way down to Baltimore. As the Winter Solstice approached, Evan stepped up his search for a way to stop the ghost and the Hunt. More than anyone else, he knew that they must be stopped before the solstice, to return the world to balance and harmony. The alternative didn't bear thinking about.

Sam had been too heartsick to return to the family Bible, but Phil had used his time as a convalescent to follow the family tree to the present. And so they learned of the fate of the nineteenth century Cartwrights, who were able to return home to Seawind. In fact, Marie's children were born there. She had married a distant cousin, and had five sons and two daughters. Her youngest son was named Edward, for her father, and *his* youngest daughter was Caroline, born in 1917.

"That would Beth's Aunt Caroline?" said Sam.

"Yes, Seawind came back to the Cartwright family after Barnaby's death," Phil was pleased to be able to share this bit of news. Barnaby's widow, whom he had treated cruelly in his lifetime, gave away all his remaining wealth and property, after his debts had been paid, to its rightful owners. With her strict Quaker beliefs, she could not abide the means by which his wealth had been gained. She then returned to her own people

in Westerly.


At this point Phil broke off to say cordially to Sebastian who had jumped up to perch

beside him on the counter, "Hey Dude, how's it goin'?" This exchange distracted Sam

from the story. "Dude?" she thought, rather irrelevantly under the circumstances, "you

call my cat Dude?" Sebastian however had no reservations about this form of address,

high fiving Phil and graciously accepting the morsel of smoked salmon he offered.

Indeed since the summoning and its inglorious ending, he had taken to spending

marked periods of time with Phil. Sam rather cynically attributed this new friendship to

the shrimp cocktails and mahi mahi Phil produced at dinner time with weekly

regularity. These were Sebastian's favorite foods.


But this evening there was something else to celebrate. Lined up neatly on the counter,

were six cut-glass dessert plates. And a familiar, delicious smell wafted from the six

small patty pans full of custard, fresh from the oven. As his audience watched with

bated breath, Phil tipped each one over.

"They turned out right!" Phil and Beth were jubilant. The caramel custards were

unbroken and divine smelling. Sam's eyes narrowed as she viewed the plates set out,

each perfect little custard decorated with a jaunty sprig of mint. Had the Hunt anything to do with this? She recalled her conversation with Max in Chinatown, which seemed a lifetime away. The Hunt is fey but not evil, he had said. And indeed, Phil took no lasting hurt from his bruising encounter. In fact, he was having a remarkable run of good luck. Her spirits lifted a little. Maybe, just maybe, they could help the Hunt capture the evil spirit of William Barnaby. She hurried to eat her share of the caramel custard before Sebastian and Daisy persuaded Phil to feed it all to them.

# 11. The Last Hunt

On the day of the Winter Solstice, Sam walked on the beach. The foaming water ran at her ankles and pieces of seaglass showed themselves half-buried in sand and weed. A long-forgotten line from a poem came back to her: "O! Is it weed or fish or floating hair...a drowned maiden's hair..." All of life and death were here on the edge of the two worlds. The crab claws and the shells that had been bits of someone's home, the seagull feathers and the tiny creatures that burrowed in the sand as each wave retreated. Life and death, eternally inseparable, make what you will of it. Studying the bits of driftwood thrown up by the winter storms, she remembered the one that she had picked on her first day - a square with nearly straight lines, messages intricately carved on its surface by water and sand. It had vanished with the first hunt. Suddenly Sam knew how the ghost had found its way from the depths of the ocean to Seawind. She also knew it was time to go home.

Her instinct was right. The folklorist was there, holding forth to Beth and Phil, who looked both nervous and skeptical. "There is another verse," said Beth, as Sam entered. "Of course, it was in the last place I would have thought of looking," Evan said thoughtfully, and, it must be admitted, complacently, "Though once found, it makes perfect sense."

"This," he continued, flourishing a yellowed piece of paper with fraying edges, "was in my grandmother's grimoire, of blood and healing. And of course, it is a sickness in the world that we need to be healing. And blood, you know, is akin to seawater."

"And also tears," Sam offered.

He looked at her sharply.

"Aye, that is so indeed."

"But doesn't it need a full moon? It's actually a moonless night out tonight."

"Which, as you know, is considered unlucky in many cultures. But it may serve our purpose."


This time they were four. They made their way cautiously along the dark path, hardly able to see each other. In the clearing by the oak tree they halted, then went forward. On the night of the winter solstice, the air was bitter cold and the trees devoid of life. Grimly they formed a circle, joining hands, and waited for the folklorist to speak. His words rang clear and full of doom:

"By Dark of the Moon,

Cross the Shore of Sorrow,

To the Wounded tree,

We Command: Stand and Speak!"

The Hunt arrived silently, in the blink of an eye. One moment there was only the darkened clearing, the next, it was full of riders and hounds. The Hunter gave off his own light that gleamed dully like a hidden moon and illuminated the Hunt, standing still and silent like a frozen nightmare. Only the occasional jingle of harness and the shifting and breathing of the horses indicated that it was not a fearsome frieze carved in stone.

Grudgingly, the antlered head acknowledged their presence.

"You are the right number," the Voice said, "The right words have been spoken."

Evan raised his eyes to the Hunter. With all his foreknowledge and experience, he found the words with difficulty.

"A good evening to you, Lord of the Hunt," he began, "and thanks for your presence here..."

The Hunter cut him off abruptly, "Neither a good even nor a good morn will it be if yon spirit maintains his freedom to work evil. Speak plain, mortal, I will naught have fancy words."


Evan tried again. He had to stop and  clear his throat before he could get the words out:

"It is plain, as you say, that the spirit runs free to do evil, and the bounds no longer hold him or the Hunt. Your duty goes unfulfilled and the Hunt strays from the paths.  It is not your part to ruin human habitation but to bring justice to the unpunished evil."

Murmurs of assent rose from the fearsome crowd.

But the Hunter replied scornfully: "Do you, Mortal, pretend to command me? Or mayhap you think to aid the Hunt? Perish those dreams, for you have not the power or wisdom for either."

He broke off abruptly, for he caught sight of Sebastian, who had just then sauntered into the clearing. A dramatic change came over him. One could not say of so fearsome a being that he became human, but the Voice softened, the Hunter dismounted and knelt. "Here, Kitty," he said, and Sebastian, unafraid, with his tail in the air and nose pointed, went forward to meet him. The Hunter placed his hand on Sebastian's head, and spoke in a low voice. As Sebastian did the little chin toss which is how he nods, the Hunter scooped him up.

Then he spoke to the four for the last time: "You speak truly, great evil has been done. It shall be amended. Our friend will guide us." Wrapping the cat in his cloak, he sprang into the saddle. From this great height, Sebastian looked down, looking insufferably smug, as only a cat can. With a great effort Sam moved, throwing herself forward to grasp the hem of the Hunter's cloak. "Wait," she cried, "not him! He's just-a-cat. He doesn't know anything. And besides, he's mine!" She missed, and fell on her hands and knees, gripping rough, cold grass. But the Hunt was gone.

# 12. The Return

The doors stayed open all night, and the lights burned in the sleepless house. The winds shrieked and howled in and around, creating little storms of paper and light objects. They didn't know where Sebastian was, and if he would ever come back. Sam sat dry-eyed at the kitchen table, her eyes on the open door. Phil tried to offer warm drinks to everyone, but the thought of food or drink was unbearable to them. Giving up, he joined Beth in her vigil in the living room. Evan had been reluctant to leave, so Beth put him in one of the empty rooms upstairs where he sat in silent thought, grey faced and withdrawn.

Some time near dawn Sam must have fallen asleep for she woke cold and stiff, trying to place the noise that had woken her. The wind was gone, and in its place was a small, persistent clinking, from somewhere high in the house. She stumbled up the three flights of steps to the attic, and there, in her room, eating busily, was Sebastian. "Bunny, you came back!" she cried, running to hug him. He squirmed and managed to convey in a civil way that he was happy to see her, but wanted to continue with his meal. He looked sleek and happy, and was wearing a pale blue velvet ribbon around his neck, with something shiny dangling from it. The clinking noise was when the shiny silver thing hit his feeding bowl, with each mouthful. Sam took a closer look, and saw that it was a small silver key. "A key," said Beth. She had followed Sam up the stairs, and in her haggard face hope dawned. "A key!" They looked at each other in wild surmise, then Sam manhandled ribbon and key off Sebastian and they were running down the stairs to the morning room where the green and silver box was kept.

When Beth picked up the box, something inside it slid sideways with a soft thump as she tried the key. There had never been a hint before of the box's contents. The key fit perfectly. The lid flung open smoothly to reveal a small rectangle of black oilskin, folded many times over. They knew somehow that this was the object William Barnaby had taken from the dying man, on a stormy beach a hundred and fifty years ago. With shaking hands Beth unwrapped the silky cover, which finally lay open to reveal a small object that gleamed dull gold. It was an intricately worked pendant flowering with inset red, green and white stones. It was not attached to a chain or necklace but hung on a worn leather strap. The strap was broken sharply and unevenly in the middle, as if pulled by an implacable hand. This was the "Persian gold" of Edward's letters, for which he had staked and lost his life. It was home at last.

There was something else hidden in the folds of waterproof oilskin, which Sam pulled out and opened carefully. A yellowing piece of parchment, folded to a small square, nearly coming apart at the the folds. Carefully spread out on the table alongside the family Bible, it revealed faded cursive writing in dark blue ink.

"Some kind of legal document?" guessed Beth, holding the golden rose in a happy daze. She didn't really care about too much else at that moment.

Sam read out the words carefully: "On this day, the 1st of February in the year 1882, herewith attested is payment made in full for the house and ship *Seawind* by Edward Cartwright to William Barnaby. There are no further debts owing."

It was witnessed by one Joshua Waterman, a notary, and had been signed by all three in Boston.


The document completed the story of Barnaby's treachery. Returning from the East, even before meeting his anxious family, Edward first went to Boston to repay his debt. But he made the fatal mistake, in his innocent pride, of showing Barnaby the necklace. The sight of the gold ignited all the greed and baseless in Barnaby's nature. Even though he had been repaid in full, he wanted the gold, and Edward refused to part with it. As Edward and *Seawind* sailed again, first for Chatham and then southwards, Barnaby hurried overland to the Cape. When *Seawind* ran aground, Edward tried to keep the gold and the receipt safe, though all else was lost. But he had not reckoned on Barnaby's treachery.

"So even though he had been repaid, Good William concealed the receipt and turned Edward's family out of the house," concluded Phil, who had joined them. He derived a certain gloomy satisfaction from this confirmation of the depths of Barnaby's evil nature.

Beth had long ago dropped her skepticism, and now only wondered why the ghost had returned to *Seawind:* "Was the necklace always in the box or did the ghost put it there? Was he still trying to steal it or to make amends to Edward's descendant?"

Sam suspected that only the Hunt knew the answers. And perhaps Sebastian.


Beth decided not to sell the golden rose but to display it. It wasn't a difficult choice, though they really needed the money. It belonged with the family, after all the hardships they had endured. But all the publicity with the ghost and the wild weather had business humming, with people driving down from as far away as New York City to dine at the Inn. The fame of Phil's cooking had spread by word of mouth; and this surge in popularity finally prompted the food channel to offer him a contract for a six-part series called "The Haunted Buffet". Someone in New York City was developing a Cape Cod sense of humor. They wanted to begin filming in May, when the TV crews would doubtless contribute their quota to the crowds, traffic and chaos. Sam hoped fervently Phil wouldn't spill, burn or otherwise destroy anything while on camera, and that he would refrain from throwing pans and dishes at the film crew. Luckily, all went well and Phil's wooden, deadpan style on camera became a huge hit. The earnings from the show enabled them to repay the mortgage in full. So it happened that another piece of folk wisdom, which held that the Hunt brought good luck to any farm where it stopped and was treated well, proved to be true.

Evan had been as glad of Sebastian's return as Sam herself. She went out to Nauset marsh one final time, to say her goodbyes. It was a clear, calm day and she walked through the salt marsh on the raised wooden path. Under the late winter sun the marsh was a vivid contrast of dull gold and brilliant blue, now tinged pink and amethyst with the approaching sunset. She then took her way to the folklorist's cottage. His hospitality this time took the form of black coffee and foresty-tasting cookies with a flavor - was it moss? or acorns? - that she could not identify but remembered for a long time afterwards.

"So the tales do not lie," he observed, restored to his normal Holmesian calm, "The Hunt did indeed bring luck and gifts of silver."

"Yes, I suppose Sebastian helped them complete their task, so they feel they were treated well at Seawind."

"The Cat," he mused, "I wonder if we shall ever hear about his journey?"

"I'll be sure to let you know," said Sam, "if he tells me."

She rose and put her mug in the sink, and having thanked and admired the cats, walked

out to the car. Old Evan accompanied her and as she prepared to start the engine, said,

"There's another legend about the Cape, you know?"

"Oh? Which one?"

"Once you've drunk the water here, you will always return."

"Maybe," said Sam, "maybe."


Sam and Sebastian were heading back to their old haunts. Though limited, royalties and

advances were trickling in, and it looked as if her career as a writer might take off.

Sebastian supervised the packing, hiding in the boxes and pouncing at her when she

passed by. As she packed her numerous books and limited worldly goods, she knew

they were both looking forward to living within twenty minutes of decent shish kebab

and sushi. She went into the living room for another armful of books to pack into the

already bulging tote bags, and stopped. Standing by the window, looking out at the

apple tree in front of the house, was an Edwardian matron. She turned around as Sam

came in, and held out her hands with a smile. Sam had seen pictures of Aunt Caroline,

and the family resemblance was strong. Marie Cartwright had returned to her domain

in peace at long last. She didn't look like a ghost though, there was nothing

insubstantial or even sepia-tinted about her. Her crisp white blouse fastened with a

cameo brooch, the curly red hair that Beth had inherited, Marie's now touched with a little grey, were as real as Sam herself. For a long moment they stared at each other, then the ghost spoke. Her voice was sweet and low, her words clear.

"You did well here, Lady," she said, "you and the Cat. We are grateful for your freeing our house of this persistent Evil."

For the life of her, Sam couldn't speak a word, but it didn't seem to matter. Marie Cartwright raised a hand in farewell, turned, and vanished. But that was not why Sam gasped out loud and clutched at the door frame for support. Hidden behind Marie's long skirts was a small black cat, who also turned, following its mistress on light dancing feet, tail waving, and vanished behind her. That was how Sam knew that her last vision of a ghost at the Inn had been not a haunting, but a benediction.

———

"So tell me," Sam said to Sebastian as they headed south along I-95 to a new life, "how come the second summoning worked, even without the moon?"

The cat kept his thoughts to himself, staring out of the window derisively at the monster tractor trailer roaring and snorting in the right lane as they sped past. He always preferred to let her work things out for herself. And it slowly dawned on Samantha that the moon is always full. It's just the light that is different.